A TEDDY BEARS' PICNIC

CECILIA KING

Illustrated by Tony Herbert

Scripture Union
130 City Road, London EC1V 2NJ

By the same author:
Andrew and the Baked Beans

© Cecilia King 1989
First published 1989

ISBN 0 86201 565 0

All rights reserved. No part of this publication may be reproduced, stored in a retrieval system, or transmitted, in any form or by any means, electronic, mechanical, photocopying, recording or otherwise, without the prior permission of Scripture Union.

Phototypeset by Input Typesetting Ltd, London
Printed and bound in Great Britain by Cox and Wyman Ltd, Reading

Contents

Andrew and the teddy bears' picnic	7
At the seaside	13
James	20
Toby's ears	26
Trees in the kitchen	33
Andrew's eyes	39
The new Scramblers' room	45
Changes	51
Building	57
Andrew and Anna	61
Andrew's sandwich	68
Andrew's bath-time	74
Andrew's difficult day	81
Splash	86
The baby	91

Andrew and the teddy bears' picnic

Andrew looked at his two teddy bears.

Snowy, the white bear, lay face down on the bed. No, he wouldn't take him, he was too special.

Sid, the black bear, was small and scruffy. Andrew didn't want to be seen with him!

'Hurry up,' shouted Mum from the kitchen. 'You'll be late for the playgroup's Teddy Bears' Picnic.'

'I can't choose,' said Andrew, slowly walking down the stairs. Mum came to the kitchen door with her hands behind her back.

'What about this?' she laughed, and produced a dark brown bear. To Andrew's surprise it waved at him.

'How did he do that?' asked Andrew.

'Say hello to him, Andrew,' said Mum.
'No!' said Andrew.
The little bear rubbed its eyes.
'You've made him cry. Please say hello.'
'Hello, bear,' replied Andrew.
'Here! Hold him. He is yours. We bought him ages ago but you kept chewing his ear, so we put him up in the loft. I'd forgotten all about him until this morning.'
'He's a big glove!' said Andrew, trying to squeeze his fingers into the right places.
'That's right. He's a glove puppet.'
'Can we go now?' asked Andrew.
'Yes. Call William in from the garden.'
Andrew flung open the back door. 'William! Willie! In!!'
William, the dog, ran into the kitchen and up to the bear. He sniffed its soft brown fur.
'Grrrrrrrrr,' growled Andrew, making the bear close its paws around the end of William's nose.
'Stop it,' said Mum.
'It wasn't me, it was him,' said Andrew.

Andrew loved the honey sandwiches, and the cold milk from the plastic cup. He looked down at his bear. His was the best. There were pink bears, red bears, blue bears and even a bright green bear, but none of them moved like his bear. All his friends wanted to stroke it and they all went 'Aaah' when Andrew made the bear hide its face in its paws.

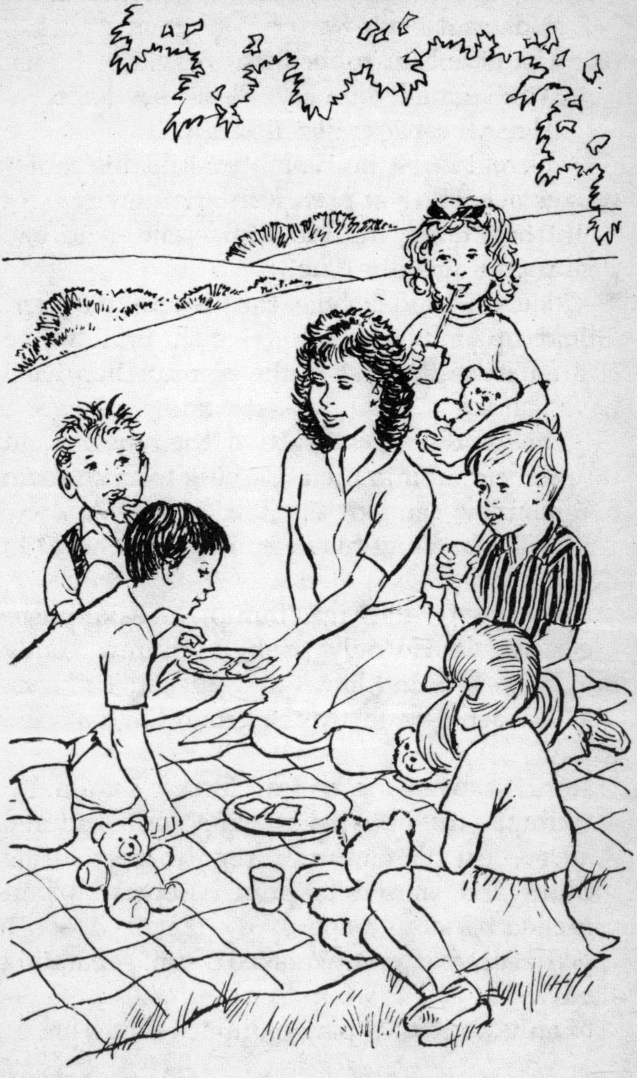

'Is he sad?' asked David.

'Yes, because he's hungry,' laughed Andrew, using the bear to snatch David's honey sandwich.

'Hey, give it back,' shouted David.

'Andrew, don't be naughty!' said his mum, who was helping at playgroup that day.

'It wasn't me, it was him,' said Andrew, pointing at his bear.

'Come on,' said Debbie, the playgroup leader. 'Stand up and play for a while, until we've cleared away the rest of the picnic. Then we'll have a story.'

Some of the boys grabbed their bears and threw them up into the air, trying to catch them before they landed on the grass. Andrew watched, clutching his bear. He didn't want to do that.

Tim came running up. 'Bump,' he said, pushing Andrew. He only pushed Andrew gently but Andrew didn't like it and pushed Tim back a lot harder. Tim fell to the ground and started to cry.

Robert saw all this and decided to join in.

'Bump!' he shouted, falling on Andrew. Andrew lost his temper, threw his bear to the ground and started to punch Robert. Robert punched back.

'What are you doing?' asked Mum, separating them.

'I only wanted to play bump,' wailed Tim.

'Come on, you three, pick up your bears and sit down on the grass with me,' said Mum.

Andrew, Robert and Tim, who was still sniffing, sat next to Andrew's mum.

'Tim's got a stupid bear,' whispered Robert to Andrew. Tim's bottom lip began to quiver.

'Don't be so horrible,' said Mum. 'You've got a lovely bear, Tim. Now tell me about this "Bump" game.'

Tim wiped his eyes. 'I play it with my big brother. He never hurts me.'

'I'm afraid Andrew thought you wanted to fight,' answered Mum.

'I did!' shouted Robert, clenching his fists.

'That's enough,' Mum said sternly.

'Tim started it,' protested Andrew.

Robert laughed.

'It's not funny,' said Mum, then she sighed, 'Robert, you were really good on Sunday morning when you said your prayer in church.'

'I don't want to be like that all the time,' sulked Robert.

Mum agreed. 'God wants you all to enjoy yourselves in many different ways. Look at the boys and girls playing.' They did. Some of their friends were running and jumping. Thomas stood quietly, cuddling his bear. Donna and Sarah were talking, and Natasha was reading a book.

'Can't we hit each other a little bit?' asked Robert.

'There's nothing wrong with rough and tumble, as long as no one gets hurt,' replied Mum.

'Andrew always gets angry,' grumbled Tim.

'That's not true, Tim. You played together yesterday morning and got on very well,' pointed out Mum. 'Perhaps it was silly of you to bump Andrew.'

All four were quiet for a minute.

'Let's play rough and tumble,' said Andrew.

'OK, but be careful,' said Mum, grabbing hold of Andrew's legs and tickling him.

'I didn't mean you. You're too old,' laughed Andrew.

All three boys got up and ran away from Andrew's mum, who chased them round a tree. Finally they fell onto the grass in a heap.

'Stop tickling,' gasped Tim.

'It's not me,' gulped Robert.

'Or me,' mumbled Andrew from underneath them both.

'It's him,' smiled Mum, holding Andrew's bear, who cheekily waved his paw and scratched his ear.

At the seaside

Andrew lay in bed trying to get to sleep. But he couldn't; he was too excited. Tomorrow morning the Scrambler Sunday School class was going to the seaside. Simon and Joanne, the Scrambler leaders, had arranged for a minibus to take them all. Andrew's dad, who was also a Scrambler leader, was going to *drive* the minibus. This made Andrew feel very proud. On the chair at the bottom of the bed were Andrew's clothes and lunch box. He had already made his sandwiches of peanut butter and raspberry jam, and they were carefully wrapped in silver foil. The blue thermos flask was filled to the top with milk, because Andrew's mum had forgotten to buy any orange juice. Andrew sighed and closed his eyes. After a minute he opened one of them again, then the other. I'm fed up, I can't sleep! he thought, sitting up in bed. The bedroom door opened, and Mum walked in.

'I can't get to sleep,' moaned Andrew.

'Oh dear, you must try, or you'll be tired tomorrow,' said Mum, picking up Andrew's Bible. 'Would you like a story?'

'Yes, please,' answered Andrew.

Mum turned to Luke chapter 5, and said, 'Jesus was standing on the shore of Lake Gennesaret. Lots of people wanted to hear what he had to say, and they kept pushing each other. Jesus saw two boats pulled up on the beach; the fishermen had left them, and were washing their nets. Jesus got into one of the boats.'

'Did the fisherman mind Jesus getting into his boat?' asked Andrew.

'No. He asked Simon Peter, one of the fishermen, to push the boat off a little from the shore. Jesus sat in the boat and everyone could see him and hear what he was saying,' said Mum. Andrew yawned.

'Do you want to hear the rest of the story?' asked Mum. Andrew nodded.

'After Jesus had finished talking to the people, he said to Simon, "Push the boat out further to the deep water, and let down your nets for a catch." Well, I don't think Simon thought this was a very good idea,' said Mum.

'Why not?' asked Andrew.

'Simon and the other fishermen had been fishing all night and they hadn't caught a thing. Still, Simon did what Jesus said, and let down his nets, and caught so many fish. Simon felt he wasn't good enough to know such a wonderful teacher as Jesus, and he fell on his knees in front of him. Jesus said to Simon, "Don't be afraid; from now on you will be catching men." '

Andrew looked puzzled. Mum smiled and said, 'What Jesus meant was that Simon Peter and his friends were going to become Jesus' special friends, and help Jesus tell everyone about God.'

Andrew closed his eyes and this time he didn't open them again until the next morning.

Outside their church the Scrambler class waited for the minibus. Toby kept running to the edge of the pavement. Once he tripped up and fell into the road. His mum told him off. Toby went and sulked on the church step. Toby's mum had offered to come with the Scrambler class, because she knew how naughty Toby could be. He was always pushing and bullying the other children.

'There's my dad in the minibus,' shouted Andrew, jumping up and down. The minibus stopped, and Simon and Joanne, the Scrambler leaders, counted all the children as they climbed in.

'Are we all ready to go?' asked Simon.

'Yes!' shouted back the Scramblers.

Andrew's dad drove the minibus carefully through the village where they lived, and out onto the main road. Andrew loved to watch the big lorries go by as Dad overtook them. One lorry driver smiled and waved, and all the Scramblers waved back. After a while though, they got bored, so when Joanne shouted, 'There's the sea!' the Scramblers were really pleased and laughed and pointed out through the window.

Andrew's dad parked the minibus near the beach, and it wasn't long before they were running around, getting sand in their shoes.

'Calm down!' shouted Joanne.

'Can I go swimming?' asked David.

'I want my sandwiches,' said Andrew, opening his lunch box.

'I found a pretty shell,' smiled Sarah, showing it to Hannah.

'Sit down and let's eat,' said Simon firmly. A few minutes later everyone was quietly eating and gazing at the waves, as they splashed onto the sandy beach.

'May I see the shell you found, Sarah?' asked Simon. Sarah leaned over to give the shell to Simon. Toby pushed her in the back and she fell forward, right on top of her sandwiches. When she sat up her hair and face were covered in sand.

'Toby!' shouted his mum, picking him up and taking him away from the rest of the group.

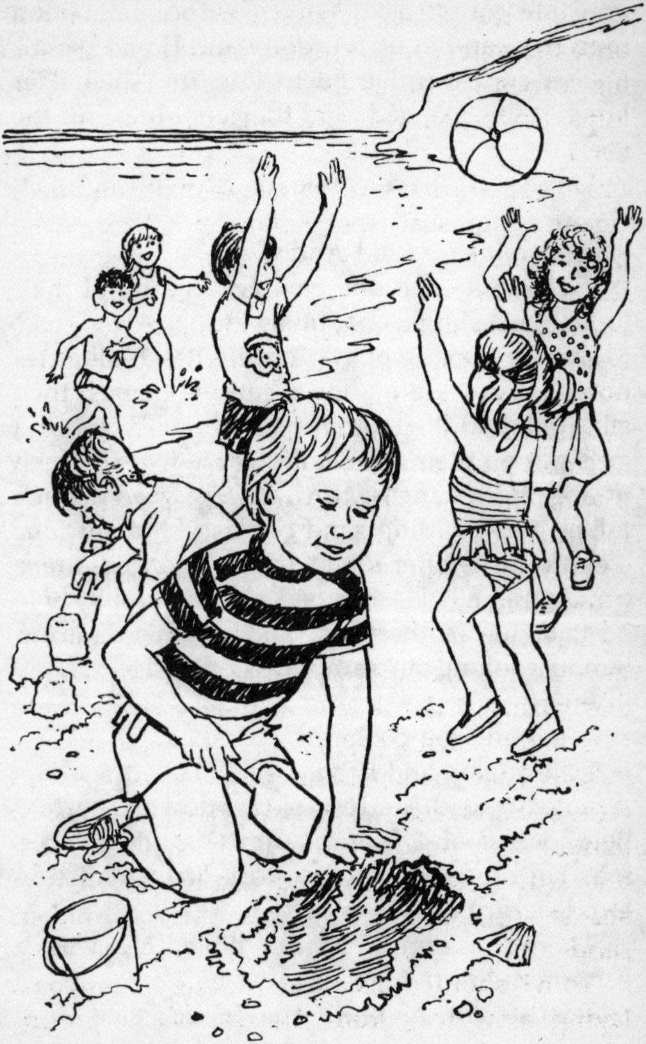

Sarah's eyes were full of tears, which dripped onto her sandy face. While Joanne and Simon tried to clean her up, Andrew and David picked up her lunch and tried to find the shell. Her lunch was squashed, and they couldn't find the shell.

'Sarah can have some of my lunch,' said David.

'And mine,' added Andrew.

In the end everyone gave Sarah a bit of their lunch, and she felt happy again.

The Scramblers played on the beach all afternoon. Simon and Joanne organised games, they all went paddling, and a few brave boys and girls put on their swimsuits. There was so much to do, finding shells, throwing seaweed at each other, and building sand castles. At about four o'clock in the afternoon, Andrew noticed a nice cooking smell. He climbed out of the big hole he had dug in the sand, and saw his dad and Simon cooking on camping stoves. He ran up to them.

'What are you cooking?' he asked.

'Fish fingers and beans,' said Dad.

'Lovely,' said Andrew, sitting down to watch. Behind Dad and Simon, Andrew could see the sea. He remembered the story Mum had told him last night.

'There's a Simon in the Bible. He was a fisherman,' said Andrew.

'That's right, he was Jesus' friend,' said Dad.

'So are you, aren't you, Simon?' smiled Andrew.

Simon laughed and said, 'Yes, but I'm not a fisherman. I just cook fish fingers!'

The fish fingers tasted better cooked in the fresh sea air. Andrew ate six!

'Time to clear up and go home,' sighed Joanne. The Scramblers made sure they didn't leave any rubbish behind on the beach. Slowly they walked to the minibus.

As Dad drove them home, Andrew thought about Jesus and his friends catching fish, cooking, and eating them by the shore. Andrew looked at *his* friends and felt happy inside.

Simon turned around and asked, 'Did you enjoy yourself today?'

'It was great,' smiled Andrew.

James

Andrew felt shy. 'Are you coming to live with us?' he asked. James, who was eleven, looked at Andrew's mum and dad.

'We hope so,' said Mum.

Andrew thought for a minute, then said, 'Do you like dogs?'

'I love them,' replied James.

'We've got a dog called William.'

'Great!' smiled James.

People called social workers kept coming to the house to see Mum, Dad and Andrew. They asked a lot of questions.

'Why do they want to know all about us?' asked Andrew.

'They want to make sure James is coming to

a good family,' said Mum.

'I'm always good,' said Andrew.

Mum didn't reply.

Dad bought a big tub of white paint and started to decorate James's bedroom. Mum made new curtains, a new carpet was laid, and a bed was delivered. It was all very exciting.

One afternoon Ryan came around to play.

'Come and see James's bedroom,' said Andrew.

'Can I come with you?' asked Dawn, Ryan's mum.

The room looked beautiful. The white walls shone in the sunlight. The carpet was bright red and covered in yellow, blue, and green stripy patterns. The bed was in the corner of the room, and on it was a red and white stripy quilt cover, and matching pillow case.

'Isn't it smart,' said Dawn.

'These are the cupboards,' laughed Andrew, pulling open the doors and jumping inside. 'James can hang all his clothes up in here.'

'Be careful, Andrew, don't lock yourself in,' warned Dawn. 'Has James seen it?' she asked.

'Not yet. He's coming to live with us on Saturday,' replied Andrew.

'Why is he living wth you?' asked Ryan, in a puzzled voice.

'The social workers said he could,' answered Andrew.

'Where's his mum and dad?' said Ryan.

'I don't know,' said Andrew.

'Why can't they look after him?' asked Ryan.

'Sometimes mummies and daddies can't look after their children,' said Dawn sadly.

Andrew got out of the cupboard and said, 'We prayed about it yesterday. Mum and Dad said that God wanted them to look after James.'

'It will be like having a big brother,' laughed Dawn.

Andrew stared at James as he ate his bran flakes. He didn't like the way he crunched them and he was using Andrew's bowl.

'Stop it!' snapped Andrew.

'What?' asked James.

'Eating!!'

Mum came in. 'Leave James alone,' she said, 'By the way, James, have you made your bed?'

'I can't remember,' said James.

'You've got a bad memory,' laughed Mum. 'You only came down five minutes ago.'

'I'll go and check,' said James, getting up from the table and running upstairs.

'Make sure you've packed your homework,' shouted Mum to James.

'Can James play football with me before he goes to school?'

'He'd better not,' said Mum. 'He'll get mud on his uniform.' James came back into the kitchen, and finished his breakfast.

'Let's play with your train set, Andrew.'

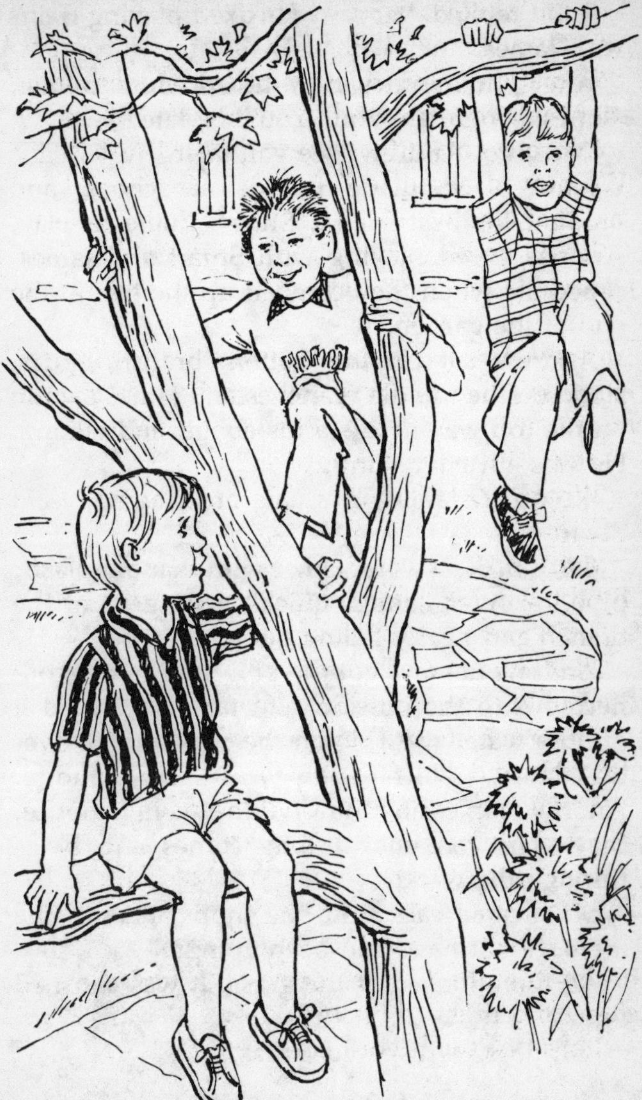

'OK,' replied Andrew. He liked playing trains with James.

After ten minutes they heard Mum calling, 'James! Where are you? You'll be late.'

'Must go, Andrew, see you later.'

James soon made friends at school, and brought his best friend, Stuart, home to play. Andrew loved playing with Stuart and James, especially when they climbed up the tree at the end of the garden.

Andrew sat on the bottom branch, Stuart stood on the middle branches and James swung on the top waving his arms about, and talking. He was always talking.

'Be quiet, James, my ears are ringing,' said Stuart.

'Let's make a water chute with that old plastic pipe,' shouted James, quickly letting go of the branch and nearly falling out of the tree.

Andrew ran and got the pipe, and James connected it to the outside cold tap. He turned it on, the water went down the pipe and all over the lawn, which soon was very muddy. Andrew, James and Stuart didn't seem to notice, they were too busy rolling stones and twigs through the water.

Mum came back from the shops and saw the mess. 'What have you been doing?'

All three looked at the grass. It was churned up.

'Oh dear,' whispered James.

'Turn that tap off at once, before you ruin the lawn!' Mum told them off.

Andrew stood listening, trying to look sorry. He was pleased God had told Mum and Dad to look after James. James was brilliant at inventing games and, somehow, being told off together wasn't as bad as being told off on your own!

Toby's ears

Toby sat in the Scramblers' Sunday School room watching the other boys and girls laughing and playing around. He couldn't hear what they were saying because his ears hurt.

Joanne, Alison and Simon, the Scrambler leaders, told everyone to stand up and go to the other end of the room.

'Toby. We're waiting for you,' called Alison.

Toby stared at his feet.

'Don't be difficult, Toby,' said Simon sternly.

They didn't know Toby couldn't hear them.

'He doesn't look well,' said Joanne thoughtfully.

'He's all right, he's just being a pain,' shouted Sam.

'He never behaves,' agreed Hannah.

'I'll get him,' said Andrew, and before anyone could stop him, he ran up to Toby and grabbed hold of his arm.

Toby looked up. He was crying.

'What's wrong?' asked Andrew, putting his arm round him.

'What are you doing?' shouted Sam crossly.

'He's ill,' answered Andrew.

All three leaders ran up to Toby.

'Is it your ears again?' asked Alison. 'I think we'd better get your mum and dad to take you home. Alison took hold of Toby's hand and led him out of the room. Simon sighed then clapped his hands.

'Let's play this game,' he said.

After the game they heard a story about Jesus, then the Scramblers sang and danced, banging drums they had made out of cardboard boxes the week before. Finally they did quiet things. Andrew carefully coloured in his picture of Jesus. Sam and Hannah finished off their model palm trees.

'Two more minutes, then it's prayer time and we'll pray for Toby,' said Simon.

'Why?' asked Sam.

'About his ears, of course,' answered Simon.

'I don't care about his ears,' said Sam.

'That's not very nice,' snapped Sarah.

'You don't like him,' said Sam.

'That's enough,' said Joanne. 'If Toby has sore ears it might explain why he's sometimes naughty.'

'I had sore ears, but I wasn't naughty,' pointed out Hannah.

'Just let's ask God to make Toby's ears better,' said Joanne.

'Yes, I want to,' whispered Sarah, remembering Toby's miserable face.

'You're soft,' hissed Sam.

Toby's mum took him to the doctor. The doctor looked in Toby's ears and said he needed to go to hospital. She gave him eardrops. Soon Toby felt better, though he complained to his mum that he could hear a lot of strange crackling and popping noises.

'Don't worry,' she smiled. 'When you're in hospital, you'll have things called grommets put in your ears, and they'll stop the noises.'

Toby didn't see how. He was frightened.

Next week Toby went into hospital. Through half closed eyes he saw the nurses walking quickly up and down the ward. His mouth was dry. What was he doing here? Where was his mum?

'Mum!'

'I'm here.'

'I want a drink,' said Toby.

'In a little while,' smiled Mum.

A nurse walked up and said 'We're ready now. Toby, you're going for a ride in your bed!'

Toby liked the ride in his bed. He was pushed

down a long passage to the place where the doctors were going to make his ears better. Toby closed his eyes and fell asleep. He felt his mum's hand holding his.

What happened next, Toby never knew, but later that day when he woke up in the children's ward of the hospital, for the first time in ages he could hear properly and those noises had gone.

'Mum!' he shouted.

'I'm here,' she answered.

'They've put those things in, haven't they?' he said.

'Yes,' replied his mum.

Toby smiled and fell asleep. When he woke up again a doctor was standing talking to his mum. She looked happy. When the doctor had gone she gave Toby a hug.

'We can go home,' she said happily.

On Sunday morning the Scramblers were busy making 'Get Well' cards for Toby.

'Do it properly,' sighed Simon, looking down at Sam's messy drawing.

'I don't like him,' muttered Sam.

'Toby's been in a lot of pain,' Simon pointed out. Sam shrugged.

'God loves Toby. He cares about him and he wants us to care about him too. Why don't you come with me to see him, and we'll take these cards and a present.'

'OK,' answered Sam slowly.

Toby was watching television. He was fed up. When he heard Simon's voice at the front door he was pleased. Simon walked into the sitting room followed by Sam, holding a large present and a pile of cards. Toby was very surprised.

'I did this,' said Sam proudly, giving Toby his card.

'I threw the first one away, and drew it again for you.' It was a drawing of a beautiful long red car, with 'Get well soon,' in large blue letters.

Toby had a good look at all the cards. He felt funny. He'd been nasty to nearly all the Scramblers class. When he saw Sarah's pretty card, he felt ashamed at the joke he'd played on her at the seaside.

'I don't want to be bad any more,' he whispered.

'Well, we're all bad sometimes,' said Simon. 'If we're *really* sorry for what we've done God forgives us.'

'Open your present, Toby,' said Sam.

Inside the wrapper was a police car and a fire engine.

'Which do you want to play with, Sam?' asked Toby.

Sam couldn't believe it. 'The police car, please.'

When Toby's mum arrived with two cups of

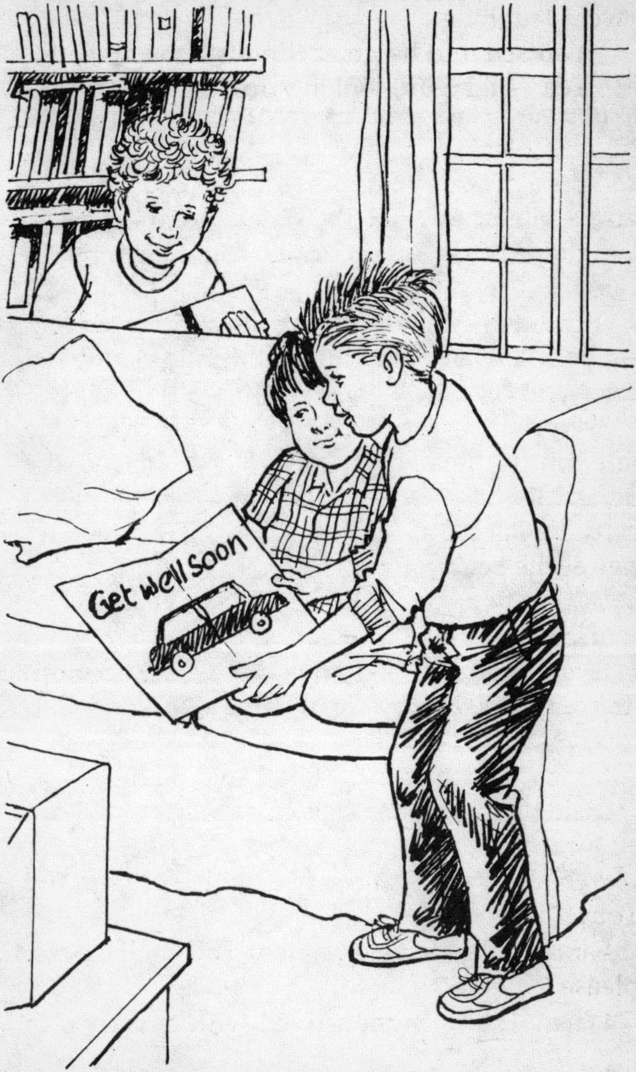
Get well soon

tea and two glasses of orange squash, both boys were laughing.

'You seem to be great friends,' she smiled.

'Yes,' said Sam, looking up, 'I think we are.'

Trees in the kitchen

'Who wants to weed the front garden?' shouted Mum.

'We will!' replied Andrew and James.

'I like weeding,' said Andrew, going into the garden shed and picking up his wheelbarrow full of his own garden tools. They had been a Christmas present from Auntie Alex.

'Don't forget your gardening gloves, Andrew,' said James, putting on a muddy pair.

'Look at my hands. Don't they look big!' James raised his hands above his head and growled, 'I'm a monster.'

Andrew picked up his rake and was just about to swing it at James when Mum arrived.

'I can see two monsters. Hurry up before the weeds choke all the flowers in the front garden.'

The two boys ran up the garden. Andrew was out of breath. He put his wheelbarrow down on the flagstones and looked at the long weedy flower bed that ran along the front of the house. He looked up over the hedge as he heard the familiar sound of a tractor rumbling past. He waved at the driver, who waved back. Andrew loved watching tractors.

'Come on, Andrew, I'm beating you,' said James, quickly pulling handfuls of weeds out and putting them in Andrew's wheelbarrow.

'Take them out of *my* wheelbarrow.'

'It doesn't matter,' answered James.

'That's *my* wheelbarrow, not yours. Get your own.'

Mum came around the corner, pushing the large wheelbarrow. 'Here we are, James, I thought you might have trouble.'

Andrew sniffed loudly and started digging out an enormous thistle. They worked hard for a few minutes and soon the weeds began to pile up. There were long stringy weeds which liked to curl around the rose bushes, nasty bindweed with large floppy white flowers, and stinging nettles.

'Oh no!' cried Andrew.

'What's the matter?' asked James.

'I've pulled up a flower by mistake.'

'Don't worry. It's an easy thing to do. We can plant it again.'

James looked down to where the flower had

been, and he saw right against the wall of the house, a small brown thing with a leaf growing out of it.

'Look at that,' he gasped, kneeling down to take a closer look. 'It's a conker with a shoot growing out of it.'

'Here's another one,' said Andrew excitedly. He gently dug it up and put it on a flagstone.

'Let's see if there's any more,' suggested James. To their amazement they found three tiny oak trees growing out of acorns.

'Orange juice for the workers,' said Mum, opening the front door.

Andrew and James were too busy concentrating on their find to hear.

'I say!' shouted Mum, 'Orange and biscuits!'

'We've found these,' smiled Andrew.

'Where?' asked Mum.

'Growing up against the wall of the house,' replied James.

'Really,' said Mum kneeling down, 'How did they get there?'

All three sat on the flagstones munching biscuits and drinking orange juice in silence, thinking how the conkers and acorns had got there.

'I remember,' said Mum smiling. 'Last autumn we went for a walk and Andrew picked up a lot of conkers from the horse chestnut trees in Hall Lane, and then we went up by the farm and collected acorns.

'I kept them in my room and *you* threw them

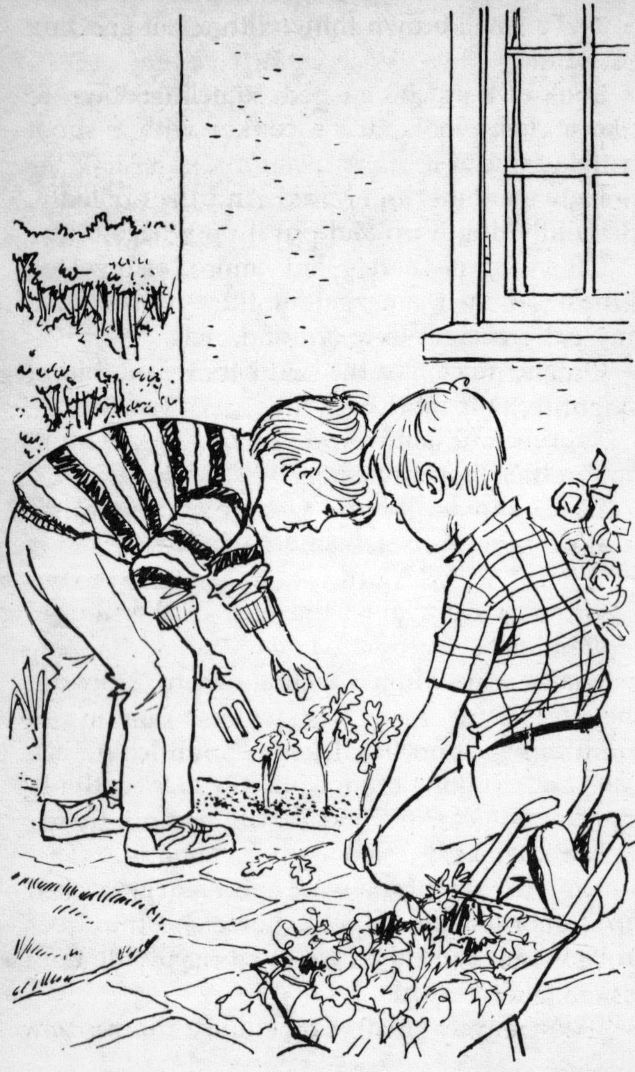

out of the window,' said Andrew accusingly.

'Only because they were on the floor and kept blocking up my hoover!' retorted Mum.

'What are we going to do with them?' asked James.

'I'd like to put them in the back garden, but our goats, Mavis and Matilda, will eat them.'

'Put them in pots,' suggested Andrew.

'They're trees,' laughed James. 'You can't keep them forever in little pots.'

'Yes, you can!' shouted Andrew.

'Calm down, please,' said Mum. 'I think we ought to look after these little trees for God.'

Andrew and James were puzzled.

'Can't *he* look after them?' asked Andrew.

'Yes, but he expects us to help by looking after and protecting plants and trees. There aren't as many oak or chestnut trees as there used to be,' said Mum sadly.

'Oh,' said Andrew slowly, 'what happens when they grow too big for the pots?'

'We'll plant them somewhere safe in the countryside,' suggested James brightly.

There was a lot of giggling when Dad arrived home from work.

'We've got five trees in the kitchen,' said Andrew cheekily.

'How am I going to get in to eat my dinner?' asked Dad.

'They're only small. Come and see,' Andrew

tugged at Dad's hand. They chased each other into the kitchen.

'See,' laughed Andrew, pointing to the window sill. There in five large pots were three oak trees and two chestnut trees.

'It's a forest!' said Dad.

'No it's not a forest, you need hundreds of trees to make a forest,' said James.

Dad sat down at the table, Andrew jumped on his lap and they had a cuddle.

'Tea won't be long,' said Mum, opening the oven door.

'Great,' said Dad, tickling Andrew until he slid off his lap.

Mum put Dad's tea on the table and Dad closed his eyes to thank God for the food. Andrew nudged him and whispered, 'Could you tell God we're looking after his trees.'

Dad opened one eye, 'I will,' he said.

Andrew's eyes

Andrew hid in the long grass of the untidy garden belonging to his house. He was playing hide and seek with his cousins Tabitha, who was eleven years old, and Luke, who was nine years old. Would they ever find him, he wondered. Suddenly Andrew saw them running down the garden. They stopped and climbed up on the old brick wall.

'I see him!' shouted Luke, pointing to a dark shape moving through the large white daisies.

Tabitha looked and said, 'That's not Andrew, that's William!' William, the dog, wagged his tail and ran up to them. Tabitha patted his long nose. Andrew giggled. How could Lukey think William was him?

Luke jumped off the wall and started to walk

through the long grass. He got closer and closer to where Andrew lay hidden. Luke stopped. He was now very close to Andrew. Andrew gently pushed his hand through a clump of blue cornflowers, and grabbed hold of Luke's foot.

'Ah, a monster's got me!' shouted Luke.

'Boo!' laughed Andrew, jumping up.

Luke and Andrew chased each other, as they ran up to the brick wall. Soon all three of them were standing on the wall gazing at the garden.

Andrew's garden was very interesting. It had a tree for climbing, near a muddy place for digging, which was by the chicken house. Every day Andrew's dad would open the chicken house door, to let out six large brown chickens, two small black chickens, and one large cockerel. Then there were the two white goats, Mavis and Matilda, who ate the grass and daisies during the day, and slept in an old building called the Coach House at night. The Coach House was in the garden near to Andrew's mum and dad's house.

Tabitha noticed something hop on to the wall next to her. It was a big green toad.

'Oh, isn't it lovely,' said Tabitha, bending down to pick it up.

'Don't pick it up, it's all slimey,' said Luke, pulling a funny face.

'It's not,' answered Tabitha.

'Let's show it to Mum and Dad,' said Andrew.

Mum and Dad were in the kitchen painting

the walls. Andrew put his head around the back door and asked.

'Can we show you something?'

'Of course,' smiled Dad, 'but be careful of the wet paint.' Tabitha and Luke walked in behind Andrew.

'What is it, then?' asked Mum, putting down her paint brush. Tabitha opened her hands and showed Mum the toad.

'Oh!' said Mum stepping back, tripping over a tin of paint and landing on the floor. 'Get it out of here!'

She didn't like toads.

Andrew was annoyed at his mum. 'It won't hurt you,' he said crossly.

'Let me see it,' said Dad, taking the toad from Tabitha.

'Please get it out of here,' pleaded Mum.

Andrew looked down at his mum sitting on the floor and said sternly, 'God made it, you know.'

Mum folded her arms and stared up at him. 'There are a lot of things God has made that I wouldn't want in *my* kitchen!'

'Come on,' said Dad, 'let's put the toad back where you found him.'

'May I have a tea towel, please?' asked Tabitha, who was kindly helping Mum up off the floor.

'What for?' asked Mum.

'I want to play the Trust game. We learnt it in Sunday Club last week.'

'OK,' said Mum.

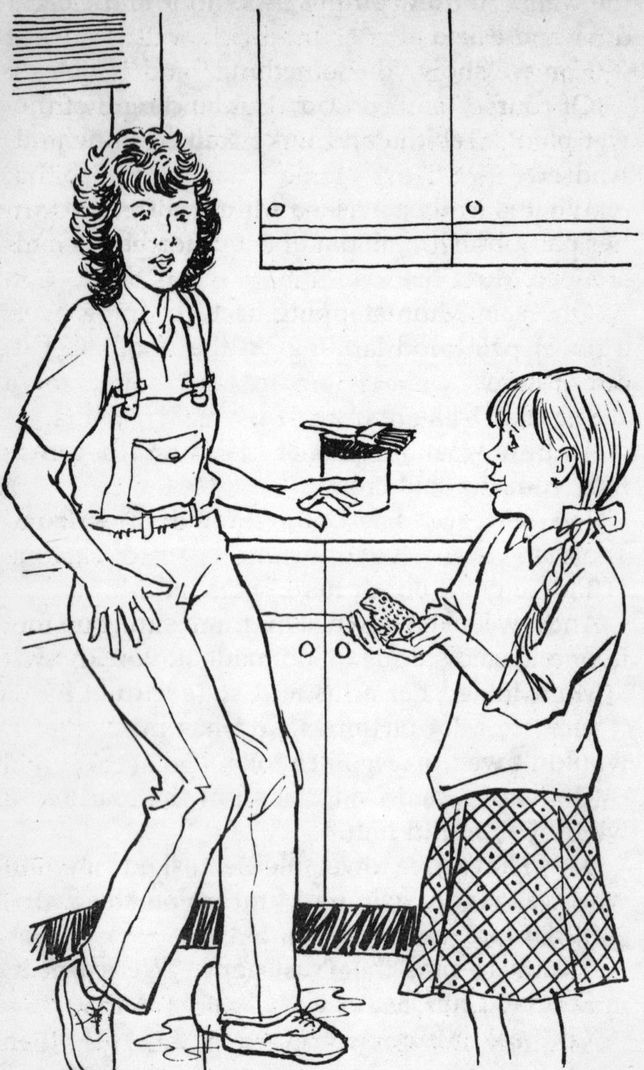

Tabitha ran out of the back door and caught up with the others at the brick wall. Dad put the toad down on the ground, and it quickly disappeared into the cool dark undergrowth.

'What shall we do now?' asked Andrew.

'Play the Trust game,' laughed Tabitha, waving the tea towel in the air. 'Luke's turn first,' she said and put the tea towel over his eyes, tying it around the back of his head. 'Can you see, Luke?' she asked.

'No,' replied Luke.

'Andrew, we're going to take Lukey for a walk, and he's got to trust us,' said Tabitha.

Andrew grabbed Luke's hand and began to pull him along.

'Careful,' said Luke, 'I'll trip over something.'

'Walk more slowly, Andrew,' said Tabitha. They led Luke along the brick wall.

'We're going down a step, so put your foot down now,' said Tabitha. Shakily Luke did what Tabitha said.

'Hurry up, Luke,' said Andrew.

'I think Andrew should have a go at this,' said Luke, and he took off the tea towel and tied it around Andrew's head.

Suddenly from being in the bright sunlight surrounded by rich green grass and beautiful flowers, Andrew was in the dark.

'Where are you?' he wailed.

'Don't worry, we're here,' said Tabitha.

Andrew felt her warm hand take his, then

Luke took hold of his other hand. Andrew walked, guided by Tabitha and Luke. Because he couldn't see, he started to listen hard to the sounds around him.

'Buzz, buzzzz,' went a bee.

'Brooom, brooom,' went a distant motorbike.

'Crunch, crunch,' went the grass underneath his feet.

The birds seemed to be singing very loudly!

'Are you all right?' asked Luke.

'We played this game at Sunday Club, before we learnt about how Jesus healed poor blind Bartimaeus,' said Tabitha.

'Mind, Andrew, there's a big stone here,' said Luke.

'Bartimaeus was waiting in a large crowd for Jesus. When he heard Jesus was coming, he began to shout for his help,' said Tabitha.

'People in the crowd told Bartimaeus to be quiet, because Jesus wouldn't want to be bothered with him!' added Luke.

'Did Jesus hear him shout?' asked Andrew.

'Yes, he did, and he made Bartimaeus see!' laughed Tabitha, taking off the tea towel from around Andrew's head.

It was wonderful to be able to see again. Andrew looked at the rambling garden with its red poppies and white daisies. Everything looked so bright after the dark.

Thank you, Father God, for my eyes, thought Andrew.

The new Scramblers' room

'I don't like this room. It smells,' said Andrew, wrinkling up his nose.

'It's lovely and big,' answered Joanne.

'Yes, but it smells,' insisted Andrew.

'Look at the view out of the window,' Simon pointed. The older members of the Scramblers class looked at the trees and grass through the window, then at the damp patch on the ceiling.

'Err, what's that?' shrieked Hannah.

'Earwigs,' said Andrew, bending down.

'I'll get rid of them,' said Simon, quickly getting a dustpan and brush.

'Let's go back to our old room,' grumbled Hannah.

'No, it's full. Isn't it great, we've had so many boys and girls joining the Scramblers, we've had to split you into two groups.'

'Why can't the other group come in here?' Andrew asked.

'They're too young. You wouldn't want little boys and girls crawling on this floor. Come and sit down on these chairs,' smiled Joanne.

Simon and Joanne started with the first activity but no one paid any attention to them.

'What a smashing cobweb,' gasped David.

'Where?' asked Andrew, jumping up.

'Next to the window. The sun's shining on it,' replied David.

'Isn't it lovely,' sighed Sarah.

'There's the spider that made it!' giggled Rachel.

Toby screamed. The Scramblers started to talk and point.

'Will you all be quiet!' snapped Simon.

'It's horrible in here!' Andrew shouted back.

There was silence for a minute.

'I'm sorry, in a few weeks time the room is to be completely redecorated. However, until then we'll have to put up with it,' said Simon.

'I'll clean it, if you want me to,' whispered Andrew.

'It's all right, Andrew, we cleaned it yesterday,' answered Joanne.

'You missed the cobweb,' laughed David.

'No, we didn't,' said Simon. 'We thought it looked too good to take down.'

Joanne looked at her watch, 'I think it's time

we got on with the story about Solomon's temple.'

Joanne told the Scramblers about King Solomon who built a beautiful building called a temple where he and his people could sing and pray to God. She described the wonderful carved wooden pillars, walls covered with golden palm leaves and jewels. Andrew looked around him at the peeling plaster, and musty carpet.

'Now,' smiled Simon, 'Let's make this room like Solomon's temple.'

The Scramblers didn't look very keen.

'Cheer up, everyone,' said Joanne, and she got out of her bag six rolls of silver foil. 'We're going to draw patterns on this,' she said.

'Why isn't it gold?' asked Hannah.

'We couldn't get any gold,' sighed Joanne.

It was fun gently scoring patterns on the shiny silver cooking foil with blunt pencils. They had to be careful not to make too many holes in it, though. As they finished, Simon and Joanne hung the foil on the walls. The room began to look a bit better. There was a knock on the door and Andrew's dad walked in. He was leading the other Scramblers group.

'Time's up! Your mums and dads are waiting for you.'

'Oh no, we haven't finished yet,' complained David.

'Just five more minutes,' begged Andrew.

Dad smiled at Joanne and Stephen and said, 'Could you come here next Saturday with the Scramblers, and completely redecorate this room with pictures and models?'

Joanne and Simon said they were free in the morning.

Dad looked at the Scramblers and asked, 'Who'd like to finish this room next Saturday morning?'

'Yes, as long as we can have orange squash and biscuits,' said Andrew.

The Scramblers worked hard the following Saturday, to make their new room look beautiful. It wasn't easy. The silver foil patterns kept coming off the walls, and in the end Joanne nailed them up.

'What are we going to use for jewels?' asked Sarah.

'Will sequins do?' said Simon.

'Yes. Aren't these sequins pretty?' said Hannah.

'I like doing this,' smiled Ben, as he finished his third picture.

'So do I,' agreed David.

By the end of the morning the room was finished. The walls glittered, the ceiling glittered, even the floor shone with dropped sequins.

On Sunday morning Andrew sniffed when he came into the room. He knelt down and sniffed the carpet. 'This smells like my mum,' he said.

Joanne laughed. 'I didn't like the musty smell when I came in here this morning, so I sprayed the carpet with my perfume spray.'

'In Solomon's temple people used perfumes to make it smell lovely,' said Simon.

'Did they have smelly carpets too?' asked Andrew.

'No,' said Joanne. 'The priests in the temple would burn a thing called incense, in special pots. The incense gave off a nice smell. When people walked into the temple and saw the wood carvings, golden palm leaves, jewels, and smelt the incense it helped them to worship God.'

'This week we'll thank God for this room,' smiled Simon.

'I think he ought to thank us for making it look good,' said Andrew.

'God is very pleased when we make pictures and models for him,' said Simon. 'In fact, Andrew, we've written a song about it. Do you want to hear it?'

'No, thank you,' said Andrew.

'We'll wait till the others arrive,' laughed Joanne.

'Do we have to do actions?' sulked Andrew.

'Yes,' replied Simon firmly. The door opened and in came the rest of the Scramblers. They sat down and happily looked at their room.

'Thank you,' smiled Simon, 'for all the pictures, models, and friezes you've made.' Then he cleared his throat and went a bit red. 'Joanne and I have written a song, and we're going to teach it to you.'

Joanne and Simon stood together and began to sing:
We make things with our hands,
We make things with our hands,
To please God, to please God.
We make things with our hands,
We make things with our hands,
To please God, to please God.

The Scramblers soon learned the song and were standing up and doing the actions. They had to point at the pictures, friezes and models they had made, dance in a circle and clap their hands. Andrew didn't usually like singing and dancing, but he felt so proud of the things he had made, that he was soon enjoying himself along with the others.'

Changes

Andrew's mum and dad looked sad. They didn't have any more money to do up their old house. They had bought the old house before Andrew was born. It was a lovely house to look at, but inside some of the walls were falling down and some of the floors weren't safe to walk on, because the wood was rotten. The roof leaked, and there wasn't a bathroom or a proper kitchen. Andrew's mum and dad had worked very hard on the old house, and slowly it was becoming a smashing place to live in. However, it cost a lot of money to fix the old house. One day Andrew's mum and dad just didn't have any left, and there was still a lot of building to do!

In their garden was a building called the Coach House. It was as old as their house.

Andrew and James loved it because they could play in it whenever it was raining. One day a man came to look at the Coach House. He nodded his head as Mum and Dad talked to him.

'Who's that?' said Andrew to James.

'That man is trying to decide whether or not we should be allowed to sell the Coach House,' answered James.

'Why?' said Andrew.

'So we can use the money to finish off our house.'

Andrew was shocked. He didn't like the idea of selling the Coach House at all! Another shock came when Dad told Andrew and James they were going to sell the goats.

'They can't stay in the Coach House, and there's nowhere else to keep them,' he said.

Andrew was angry.

The next day a van came to collect the goats, Mavis and Matilda. Andrew watched as they trotted up the ramp into the van, chewing. Mum told Andrew they were going to be well looked after in a large field. Andrew didn't care, he'd miss them. He quickly wiped away a tear.

That evening, Dad said, 'What would you like to pray about tonight?'

'I'm not talking to God,' said Andrew.

'Why not?' asked Dad.

'It's God's fault the goats have gone!' shouted Andrew angrily.

'No it's not,' sighed Dad.

'When is the lorry going to come and pick up the Coach House?' whispered Andrew.

Dad couldn't believe his ears, and before he could stop himself he began to laugh. Andrew hated being laughed at.

'Sorry I laughed at you, Andrew,' said Dad, 'but we can't move the Coach House. When it is sold and rebuilt, people are going to live next door to us.'

Andrew was confused and upset at all the changes going on around him.

'Now let's pray,' said Dad.

'No,' said Andrew, 'I don't want to.'

Andrew was looking forward to his birthday, which was the next week. His mum and dad had promised him a proper birthday party, and all his friends were coming. Every night before he went to sleep, Andrew thought about the presents he was going to get. When Dad tried to explain what was going to happen to the Coach House and some of their garden, Andrew wouldn't listen, and he still refused to talk to God.

The day of his birthday arrived. Andrew sat surrounded by his friends, who were all smiling at him. His birthday cake was in the shape of a train. He loved trains. Andrew liked watching them on television, riding on them when he went to see his Nanny, and now he was going to eat a cake train!

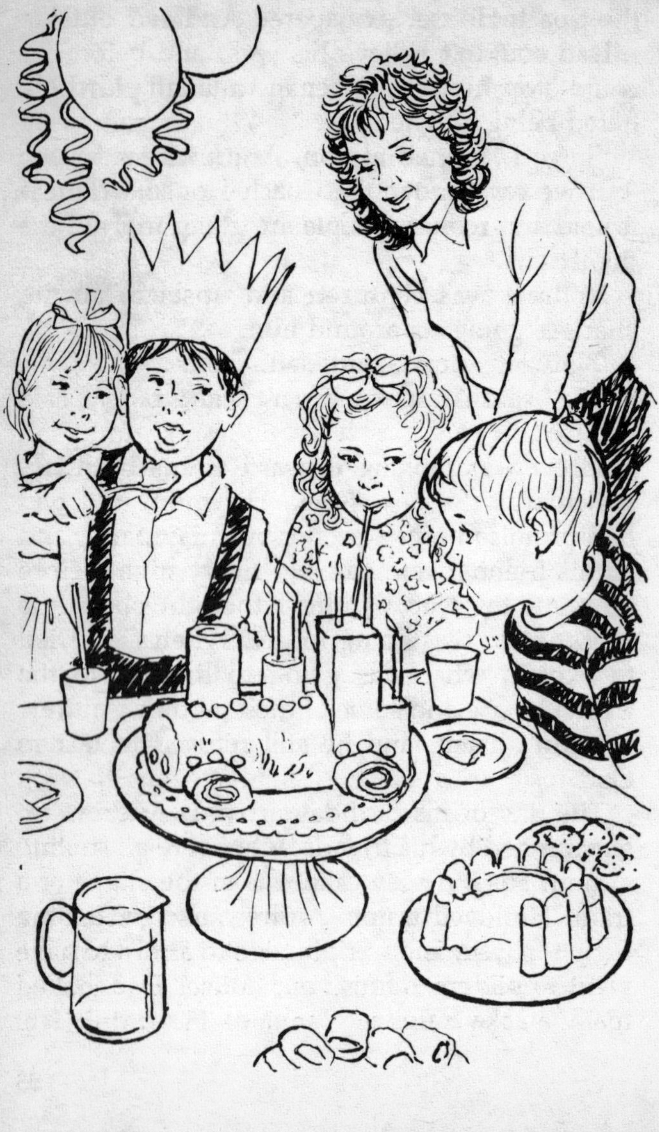

'Blow out the candles,' said Mum.

After they had eaten, everyone ran outside into the garden.

'Let's go into the Coach House and play hide and seek!' said Andrew. While they were hiding, Dad came into the Coach House with a man and a woman. He started to show them around but stopped when he heard all the giggling.

'What are you doing in here?' asked Dad.

'Playing,' shouted Andrew.

'Andrew! Meet our new neighbours.'

'We won't be moving in straight away,' said the man. 'I've got a bit of building to do.'

Andrew stared at the man and woman. They looked quite nice.

That night Dad asked Andrew, 'Did you enjoy your birthday?'

'Yes.'

'Are you still not talking to God?' asked Dad.

'I miss Mavis and Matilda,' whispered Andrew.

'I know, but you can't blame God for that. Perhaps Mum and I shouldn't have bought them at all. We took on too much when we came to live here.'

'It was fun though,' smiled Andrew.

'Yes and we'll soon have the money from the Coach House, and we'll be able to afford to have proper builders to finish our house!' Dad looked really happy. Andrew smiled. He didn't feel angry any more.

'I'm sorry I stopped talking to God,' he said.

'You know God will forgive you if you're really sorry,' smiled Dad.

'Does God get fed up with me?' yawned Andrew.

'I don't know,' said Dad, drawing the curtains, 'But I do know that he doesn't stop loving you, and he always listens to your prayers. Shall *we* talk to him now?' asked Dad, turning towards Andrew. But Andrew had fallen asleep.

Building

One Monday morning, Stephen and Kevin, the builders, started work on Andrew's house. Dad and Mum were very pleased at the thought that someone else would be doing all the building work. Andrew loved to watch Stephen and Kevin working on his house. He watched them take out the old window frames and put new ones in. He couldn't believe it when they pulled the old staircase down.

'Well,' said Mum, 'it was rotten.'

The whole family moved to live at the back of the house, so that they wouldn't get in Stephen and Kevin's way.

One morning there was a terrible crash. Andrew and his mum ran to see what had fallen down. Kevin was sitting on a pile of bricks, looking a bit dazed.

'What happened?' asked Stephen.

'I was knocking a few nails into the side of the chimney, when the middle of the chimney collapsed!'

'Oh dear,' said Stephen.

'I'll put the kettle on, and make us all a cup of tea,' said Mum.

They stood looking at the mess in the dining room. There was dust everywhere.

'It looks like we'll have to build another chimney,' sighed Stephen.

In the afternoon Andrew sat next to his mum on the couch in the sitting room.

'I know a Bible story about building,' said Mum. 'It's in Luke chapter 6 and it starts at verse 46.' Andrew listened as Mum read, ' "Why do you call me Lord, Lord, and yet don't do what I tell you? Anyone who comes to me and listens to my words and obeys them – I will show you what he is like." '

'This isn't about building,' said Andrew.

'Yes, it is, listen,' said Mum. ' "He is like a man who, in building his house, dug deep and laid the foundation on rock. The river overflowed and hit that house but could not shake it, because it was well built." '

'There's no river near us, is there?' asked Andrew, looking worried.

'No,' answered Mum.

'I know this story!' laughed Andrew. He

jumped up and sang, 'The foolish man built his house upon the sand!'

'Excuse me,' said Mum. 'May I carry on reading?'

'OK,' said Andrew, sitting down.

' "But anyone who hears my words and does not obey them is like a man who built his house without laying a foundation; when the flood hit that house it fell at once – and what a terrible crash that was!" '

'Just like your chimney,' said Stephen, who had come in while Mum was reading.

'Our chimney is very old,' pointed out Mum.

'Yes, but it wasn't built very well. I'm surprised it hasn't fallen down before!' said Stephen.

Just before lunch Kevin asked Andrew if he'd like to do a bit of plastering.

'Yes, please,' answered Andrew.

Kevin showed him how to mix the plaster and then how to spread it. Andrew was so excited that he didn't listen properly. He loved the way the plaster slopped onto the wall, and ran down onto the floor. When Andrew had finished, it looked all right, so he went happily off to have his lunch.

'Andrew, what's this?' shouted Kevin.

Andrew ran into the dining room where he'd been plastering, and saw that all his plaster had fallen off onto the floor.

Mum laughed. 'You didn't listen and look

what happened.'

Andrew went out into the garden to sulk.

In the afternoon Mum decided to try out a new cake recipe. It was called Lemon Surprise. She had just started making it when her friend Carol arrived. Andrew noticed that Mum was so busy talking that she was not concentrating.

'Mum, be careful,' he said.

'I am,' snapped Mum.

Andrew went into the sitting room and played with his railway. An hour later, Mum called him into the kitchen.

'See, here's my Lemon Surprise,' she said.

'That looks nice,' said Stephen and Kevin hopefully.

'You can have a bit when it cools,' smiled Mum.

All of a sudden the cake made a funny hissing sound, and turned from a light airy sponge into a flat pancake.

'Whoops,' said Mum, going red.

'Just like the chimney,' laughed Stephen.

'And the foolish man's house,' said Andrew.

Anna and Andrew

Anna and her mum and dad moved into a house near the church where Andrew and his mum and dad went. One Sunday morning Anna's parents decided to go to the church. Anna was put into the Scramblers' class, led by Joanne and Simon. She felt a bit nervous, because she didn't know anyone. Sarah said she could sit next to her, and she helped Anna find the best pencils when they coloured in a picture of Jesus. Anna thought the boys in the class were a bit noisy, but the girls seemed very friendly, all except Emma who said that Anna's picture was a mess.

When it was time to go home, Joanne opened the door of the Scramblers' room to let in the parents. Anna's mum and dad were the first to come in.

'Did you enjoy yourself?' asked Anna's dad.
Anna nodded.

Anna's mum was talking to Andrew's mum and they seemed to be gettng on very well.

'This is Andrew,' said his mum, pointing to him, as he busily put away the chairs.

'And this is my Anna,' smiled Anna's mum. Then she said 'Would you and Andrew like to come and have lunch with us on Wednesday?'

'I'd love to,' answered Andrew's mum.

Andrew and Anna stared at each other.

It was raining on Wednesday morning, but that didn't stop Andrew putting on his raincoat, and wellington boots, and going down to the end of the garden, to dig a hole. He'd been working on it all week, and it was now quite big and deep. The rain filled the bottom of the hole. Andrew was pleased; he pretended the sticky mud was cement.

'Andrew, come in!' shouted his mum.

'No! I'm busy,' answered Andrew.

'We're going to have lunch with your new friend!' shouted Mum.

'Who's that?' asked Andrew, puzzled.

'Anna,' replied his mum.

'She's not my friend, she's a girl,' complained Andrew.

'Hurry up, Andrew, or we'll be late,' said Mum, going back inside the house.

Although Andrew sulked, and got changed into his clean dry clothes very slowly, it wasn't long before they were ready to leave. It was a short walk to the house where Anna lived. Andrew dragged his feet.

'We'll be late,' said Mum.

'I want to be in my hole,' grumbled Andrew.

They crossed a busy main road, then walked up to a row of smart new houses and knocked on the one with the bright red door. Anna's mum opened it and smiled.

'Come in,' she said. 'Hello, Andrew. Anna's upstairs, why don't you go and play with her?'

Andrew sighed. He didn't want to play in a girl's room. He undid the zip of his jacket and gave it to his mum. Mum bent down and whispered, 'Will you cheer up'.

Anna was sitting on her bed reading a book, when she heard Andrew coming upstairs. The door to her room was wide open, so it was easy for Andrew to find it. Anna felt shy when Andrew walked in. He didn't look very friendly. Anna missed her old friends, and she missed her old house. She'd felt all horrible inside, since she'd moved. Anna knew she ought to ask Andrew what he'd like to play with. Her mum had suggested they could use the Play-Doh as long as they didn't make a mess.

Andrew thought, this isn't going to be any fun at all. He put his hands in his pockets. Anna looked very pale, she stood up and started to speak. Her voice trembled and tears began to run down her face. Oh no! She's crying, thought Andrew, and he ran to the top of the stairs. He'd better tell his mum. Then something stopped him. Why couldn't *he* ask Anna what was wrong? He turned around and went back into the bedroom. Anna sat hunched up on the bed.

'What's wrong?' asked Andrew.

'I feel sad,' answered Anna, wiping her face with the back of her hand. 'I don't like this new house, I want the old one back.'

'I love my house,' said Andrew, sitting down next to Anna. 'I'm digging this hole at the end of the garden, it's really good.'

'Are you?' said Anna, looking at Andrew. 'I was making my own tree house, but I had to leave it when I came here.' Anna began to look sad again.

'I've got a tree house, you can come and play in mine,' said Andrew.

Anna smiled. She caught sight of her face in the mirror and it was all red and blotchy.

'Yuk,' she said, then she had an idea. 'Do you like face painting?'

'Don't know,' said Andrew, looking a bit worried.

'Let's paint our faces and give our mums a shock!'

Andrew liked that idea.

Anna jumped off the bed and ran to her play-box. She opened the lid and on top of a pile of

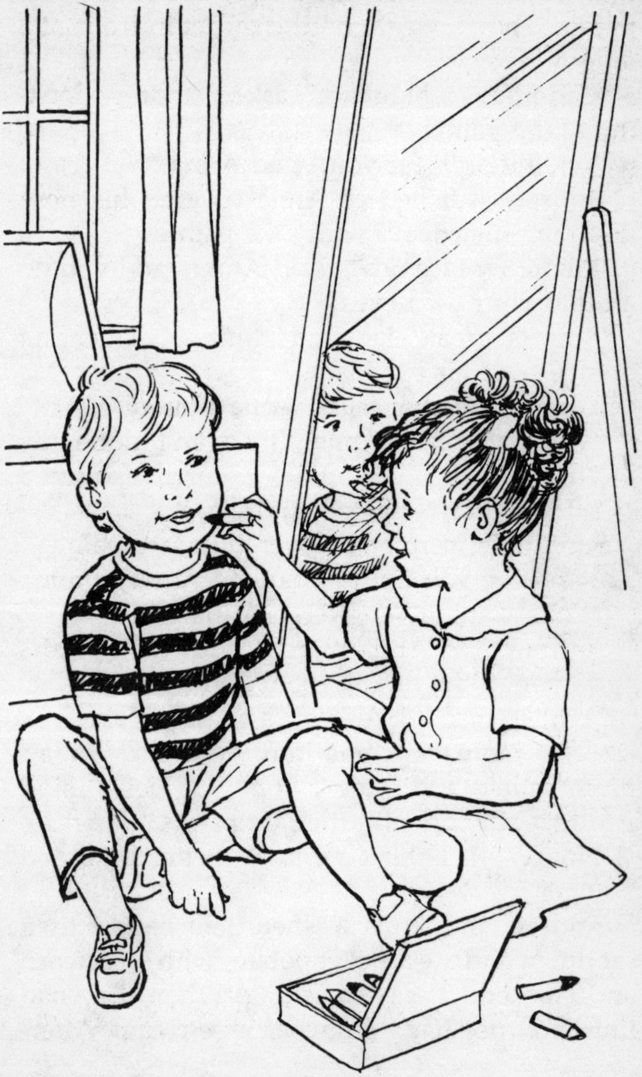

dressing-up clothes, was a colourful box of face paints. They both sat on the carpet in front of a long mirror.

'Can I have a blue face?' asked Andrew, looking at the paints.

'Yes, I'll do it for you,' said Anna.

Andrew watched as Anna covered his nose and then his cheeks with blue paint.

'I'll do my face now,' said Anna. 'and you do around your own eyes.'

'This is great,' laughed Andrew', smearing orange over his eyelids.

'Dinner's ready!' called Anna's mum.

'Oh dear,' said Anna, 'I haven't done my mouth.'

'I'll help you,' giggled Andrew.

Soon they were both covered in face paint.

'What are you up to?' shouted Anna's mum.

'We're coming!' answered Anna.

Andrew and Anna marched down the stairs and opened the dining room door.

'Arh!' screamed Andrew's mum as she saw the two monsters come into the room. Anna's mum smiled and said, 'I hope you don't mind Andrew playing with the face paints?'

'Not at all, I think he looks better blue and orange!'

Andrew and Anna washed their hands, then sat down and ate a jacket potato, with sweetcorn and chicken. It was smashing. When they had finished, they had a strawberry ice-cream. Afterwards Andrew and Anna washed their faces and played with the Play-Doh, until it was time for Andrew and his mum to go home.

On the way home Andrew said, 'I like Anna, I helped her.'

'Did you?' asked Mum. 'How?'

Andrew told his mum everything that had happened. Mum thought very hard, then to Andrew's surprise said, 'It was God who told you to speak to Anna.'

'Why do you say that?' asked Andrew.

'When you talked to Anna, it was God who helped you find the right things to say. Her mum could have stopped her crying, but she still would have felt lonely without her friends. You showed her you liked her, and now she can begin to feel wanted by the boys and girls of her own age around here.'

Andrew felt pleased God had wanted him to do something for him.

'Can I help God again?' asked Andrew.

'Yes,' replied Mum.

'When?' he said.

'Well, I'm sure it won't be long. If you keep talking to him, and listening to the stories from the Bible, it will help you to get to know God better.'

'When I get home, I'm going to finish my hole,' said Andrew. 'Oh! Will God know where I am?'

'I'm sure he will,' smiled Mum.

Andrew's sandwich

Andrew sat in his tree house at the bottom of the garden. Beneath him was James, Andrew's twelve-year-old foster brother, and James's friend, Stuart. They were swinging on the low branches of the tree.

'I'm hungry,' said Andrew.

'I'm starving!' shouted James.

'Mum promised we could have sandwiches out here this morning,' said Andrew.

'Great! I'll go and ask her if we can have them now,' smiled James, as he jumped off the branch onto the grass. Andrew and Stuart watched James run up the garden. One of Andrew's dad's chickens scratched at the earth at the foot of the tree.

'How many chickens have you got, Andrew?'

asked Stuart.

'Ten, I think,' sighed Andrew. 'I wish James would hurry up.' Andrew looked to see if James was coming, and to his surprise he saw Simon, his Scrambler leader at church. He was helping James bring the sandwiches, biscuits and drinks.

'Simon, Simon! Look at me!' yelled Andrew.

Simon waved, and when he reached the tree he offered Andrew a sandwich. Andrew took the sandwich and looked inside.

'I'm not eating that, it's cheese and pickle,' said Andrew, throwing it onto the ground. Three chickens came running up and began eating it.

'Andrew, that was *very* naughty!' snapped Simon.

Andrew was shocked. It was usually only his mum and dad who talked to him like that.

'That's a waste,' went on Simon.

'The chickens ate it,' answered Andrew.

'You didn't throw it on the ground for the chickens, you threw it away because you didn't want it.' Andrew knew Simon was right.

'Have a ham and pickle sandwich, Andrew,' said James, trying to calm them both down.

'I'm not eating anything. I'm going inside,' said Andrew.

Andrew climbed down the tree, and stomped up the garden, into the house. Mum and Dad were in the kitchen looking at posters and magazines.

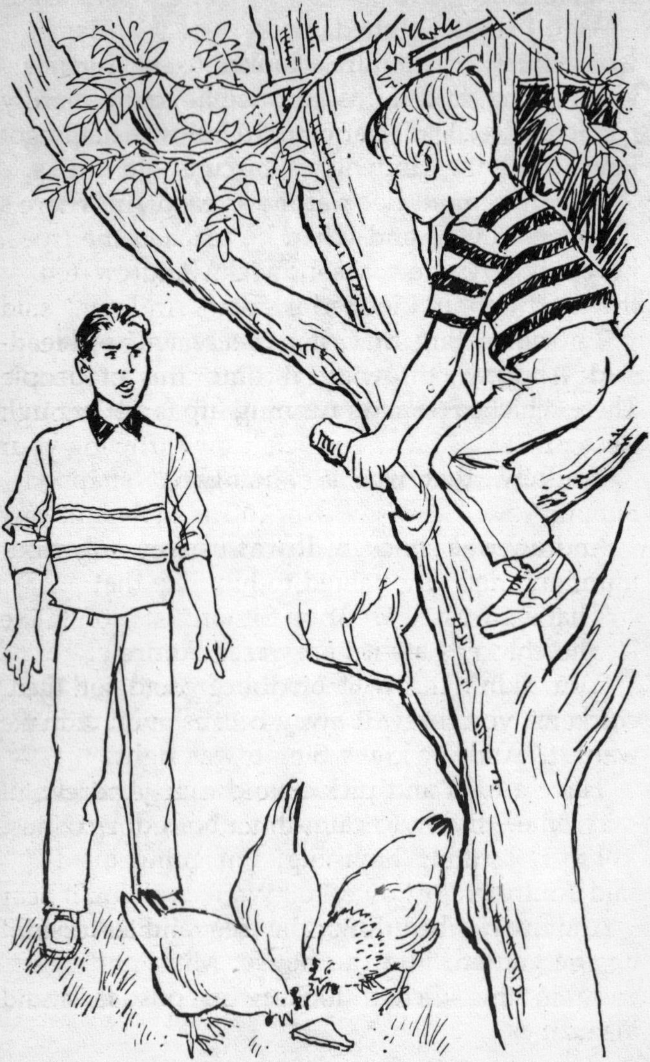

'Hello, Andrew, what's wrong?' said Dad, looking at Andrew's face.

'I don't like Simon any more,' said Andrew.

'Pardon?' said Mum, who could hardly believe her ears. Simon and Andrew usually got on well.

Simon opened the back door. 'Where's Andrew?' he asked.

'Sulking in the corner,' said Mum.

'I'm sorry I snapped at you, Andrew,' said Simon. 'You see, your dad and I have been reading about, and looking at, pictures of people who live in countries where there is not enough to eat. When I saw you just now throwing your sandwich away, it made me angry.'

Andrew wandered over to the table and saw that the magazines and posters were all about hungry, starving people.

'I'm sorry,' said Andrew. 'I just don't like cheese and pickle sandwiches.'

'Come and sit down, both of you,' said Dad. 'Eat the sandwiches you do like, and I'll make some tea.'

After lunch Andrew noticed a large picture of a boy about his own age among the magazines.

'Who is that?' he asked.

'That's a little boy called Wani, and you'll hear all about him in this Sunday's Scrambler lesson,' said Dad.

'Tell me about him now, please,' said Andrew.

'If you hear the story now, you'll be bored on Sunday,' said Dad.

'I won't,' promised Andrew.

'All right, then,' smiled Dad.

Andrew sat and listened while Dad told him about Wani, who lived in a hot country far away. Wani played outside his house, on the dusty main street of a small town. Every day he watched people coming into town from the forest. They looked tired and weak. They had had to leave their villages, because soldiers had burnt their houses, and burnt the crops they were growing in the fields. Wani didn't know why the soldiers did these awful things, he just knew that the people who came to his town were very hungry. At first Wani's mum and her friends tried to feed the people. However, slowly Wani's town ran out of food. Andrew stared at the drawing of Wani, and Wani seemed to look straight back. Wani was no different from Andrew except that Andrew had plenty to eat, and Wani didn't. Andrew felt so sad he thought he was going to cry.

Simon saw Andrew's sad face and said, 'God wants us to pray for Wani and his friends, and we can help by sending money to the people who buy food and supplies to feed the poor and hungry in the world.' Andrew nodded and felt a bit better.

Simon stood up and stretched, 'I think I'll climb your tree now,' he laughed.

'I'll race you,' said Andrew, opening the back door. Outside were the chickens pecking at the grass, and James and Stuart playing about and waving at him. Andrew rushed out of the door and into the bright sunlight.

Andrew's bath-time

Andrew had a Bible. He couldn't read it yet, but he liked looking at the pictures. Mum read him stories from his Bible. She didn't always read exactly what was written. Sometimes she would explain certain things in the story, which Andrew might find difficult to understand. Or she sometimes gave the people in the stories funny voices to make Andrew laugh. Andrew's favourite story from the Old Testament was Jonah.

'Tell me the story of Jonah,' said Andrew one evening as he lay in his bath playing.

'When you get to bed,' replied Mum.

'Why not now, when I'm in my bath?' asked Andrew.

'All right,' laughed Mum. 'I'll just go and get

your Bible.'

While Mum got Andrew's Bible, Andrew lay flat in the bath and blew bubbles in the water.

'Are you ready to listen?' said his mum, tickling his foot.

Andrew sat up and Mum began to read, 'God told Jonah to go to the city of Nineveh, and tell the people that God was very angry at the way they were behaving.'

'Were they really bad?' asked Andrew.

'Yes they were,' answered Mum. 'God was going to punish them by destroying them and their city, if they didn't say sorry to him and stop doing bad things.'

'They *must* have been bad,' said Andrew.

Andrew pushed his yellow plastic boat through the water. Then he put a little plastic man on the deck.

'This is Jonah,' he said.

'Did Jonah go to Nineveh, Andrew?' asked Mum.

'No,' smiled Andrew. Andrew knew this because he had heard the story so often.

'Yes, that's right, he caught a boat going to Spain, which was in completely the opposite direction to Nineveh. He thought the people of Nineveh were not worth saving.'

Andrew pulled his yellow boat through the water and the plastic man fell over. Then Andrew made waves in the bath. The water splashed onto the yellow boat.

'God sent a strong wind on the sea,' read Mum. 'The storm was so violent that the ship was in danger of sinking. The sailors were terrified and cried out for help.' Andrew put more plastic men on his boat and made even higher waves.

'Careful, Andrew, you're splashing me,' said Mum, as water slopped over the side of the bath.

'The captain of the ship found Jonah asleep in the bottom of the boat,' said Mum. 'He woke Jonah up, and asked him to pray to his God for help. Jonah knew God had caused the storm because he hadn't obeyed God. In the end Jonah told the sailors it was all his fault, and the best thing they could do was to throw him into the sea, and the storm would stop.'

'At first the sailors wouldn't do it, and they tried very hard to row to the shore. However, the storm got worse.'

Andrew sat all the plastic men down and made it look as if they were rowing. Then he made more waves.

'At last the sailors realised that the only way to save the ship and themselves was to throw Jonah overboard,' said Mum.

'Great!' giggled Andrew, and he threw his plastic Jonah into the bath water.

'Jonah sank into the sea, and he must have thought he was going to drown, but God commanded a large fish to swallow him, and he was

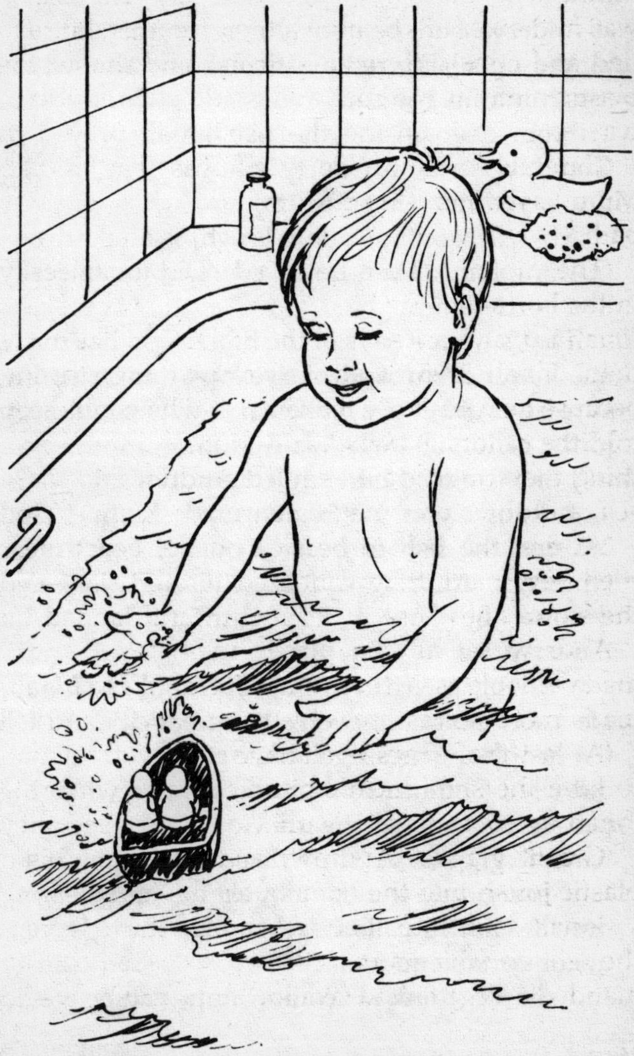

inside the fish for three days and nights,' said Mum.

Andrew had been waiting for this bit. He picked up a large red plastic fish and shoved his Jonah into its mouth.

'From deep inside the fish Jonah prayed to God and said how sorry he was that he had disobeyed him,' read Mum.

'My fish won't swallow Jonah,' said Andrew, pushing hard. Then he asked, 'Did Jonah really live inside a fish?'

'That's what it says in the Bible. God has made many wonderful and marvellous things, so I'm sure he could easily make a fish who could keep Jonah inside its belly,' said Mum.

'I like the next bit,' smiled Andrew.

'I know you do,' answered Mum. 'God ordered the fish to be sick on the beach near Nineveh.' Andrew squeezed his red fish, and the man flew out of its mouth and landed on the soap.

'Once again,' read Mum, 'God spoke to Jonah. He said "Go to Nineveh, that great city and tell the people the message I have given you." Jonah did what God had told him to do, and when the people of Nineveh heard God's message they were really sorry. They decided to show God how sorry they were by not eating, and wearing special clothes called sackcloth, which is very uncomfortable to wear.'

'I don't think I could stop eating,' said

Andrew.

'Well, they probably didn't feel like eating, knowing God was so angry with them,' said Mum thoughtfully. 'God saw what they did, he saw that they had given up doing bad things. So he changed his mind and did not punish them as he had said he would,' she finished..

Andrew picked up his Jonah and put him in the pot plant which was on the window shelf, just above the bath.

'Jonah's sulking,' said Andrew.

'Yes, he wasn't very pleased with God. Jonah thought God should destroy them all anyway even though they were sorry for what they had done. Jonah left the city and went up into the hills to watch what God would do next,' said Mum.

'It became very hot where Jonah was sitting so God made a plant to grow up and shade him from the sun. Jonah was very pleased with the plant. But at dawn the next day, at God's command, a worm attacked the plant, and it died. The sun beat down on Jonah and he became very miserable and angry. God said to Jonah, "What right have you to be angry about the plant?" Jonah replied, "I have every right to be angry!" '

'Isn't Jonah rude to God!' said Andrew. He was shocked; he would never talk to God like that.

'I know,' said Mum, and went on reading.

'God said to Jonah, "This plant grew up in one night and disappeared the next. You didn't do anything for it and you didn't make it grow – yet you feel sorry for it! How much more then, should I have pity on Nineveh, that great city which is full of people and their animals!" '

'That's right,' said Andrew, snatching up his Jonah from the pot plant and throwing him on the bathroom floor.

'It's a good job God is more patient than you!' laughed Mum, putting the Bible down and picking up Andrew's blue towel.

'I don't know why God put up with Jonah,' said Andrew, climbing out of the bath.

'He loved him,' said Mum, kissing Andrew on the cheek.

'Does he love me that much?' asked Andrew.

Mum looked down at Andrew and said, 'Yes, God loves everyone that much.'

Andrew's Difficult Day

'Leave me some,' shouted Andrew as he ran downstairs in time to see James pour out his third bowl of honey cornflakes.

'I'm hungry,' complained James.

Andrew looked inside the box. It was nearly empty!

'They're all gone!' he said.

'No, they're not,' said James.

Mum walked in, looking very pale and tired.

'There's plenty of branflakes.'

'I don't want branflakes,' grumbled Andrew.

'I'm off to school,' said James.

'Have you made your sandwiches?' said Mum.

'Yes,' said James. 'Bye.'

'Andrew,' sighed Mum, sitting down, 'could

you get me some milk from the fridge?'

'No!'

'Please, I don't feel well this morning.'

'I don't want to,' replied Andrew, then waited to be told off. To his surprise his mum slowly stood up and got the milk without saying another word.

Later, Mum took Andrew to playgroup. Outside the Village Hall the mums were waiting with their children to be let into playgroup. Andrew couldn't help overhearing David's mum asking his mum if she felt any better. Mum said she didn't and smiled.

'Have you got a stomach bug?' asked Andrew.

Some of the other women near his mum looked down at him and giggled. The door opened and they all went in.

At lunchtime Mum and Andrew sat at the kitchen table trying to decide what to eat for dinner.

'Baked beans?' suggested Andrew. Mum shook her head.

'Chicken soup?' said Andrew.

Mum started to look really ill.

'Ham?' smiled Andrew.

'Fish fingers,' whispered Mum. 'We'll have fish fingers.'

While they were eating, Andrew looked at his mum. What was wrong with her? She looked such a mess. Her hair was sticking up, and there were dark patches underneath her eyes. Mum dropped a cup. Andrew thought to himself, I'll drop my plate. Mum can't moan at me, because she dropped her cup first. Andrew elbowed his plate off the table.

'Andrew, be careful,' said Mum.

'You weren't careful,' snapped Andrew.

He was worried about his mum. The trouble was, being worried made him bad tempered and naughty. William, the dog, walked over to Andrew's plate and sniffed it.

'Leave it alone, William,' said Mum.

'Look Mum, he's dropping fur everywhere,' said Andrew. It was the time of the year when William's coat started to moult.

'Let me do the hoovering,' said Andrew, jumping up.

'If you want,' sighed Mum.

Andrew hoovered the dog hairs up from underneath the table. Then he went to hoover near the bookcase.

'Mind the vase, Andrew,' said Mum.

'Don't worry, I know what I'm doing,' replied Andrew.

Crash! The vase fell off the bookcase, and broke into two pieces on the floor. The telephone rang, 'Turn the hoover off, Andrew!' shouted Mum, as she picked up the receiver. Andrew did, then waited for his mum to finish talking to her friend.

He began to get fed up. Would she ever stop talking? I'm going to turn the hoover back on, thought Andrew. He pressed the switch, and turned his back on his mum.

'Turn it off!' shouted Mum.

Andrew ignored her and carried on hoovering. In the end Mum put down the telephone, unplugged the hoover and smacked Andrew. Tears ran down Andrew's face. He glared up at his mum, and was shocked to see she was crying too!

Mum went into the kitchen and made a pot of tea. Andrew watched the stream rise from his cup of tea.

'Can I have two spoons of sugar, please?' he asked.

'As a special treat,' replied Mum.

They sat together on the couch in the sitting room. 'Sorry,' whispered Andrew. He felt ashamed. He knew Dad wouldn't be pleased with him being nasty to Mum when she was ill.

'I'm sorry too,' said Mum.

They drank their tea.

'Do you like babies?' asked Mum.

Andrew was puzzled.

'David's got a baby brother, and so has Ryan,' went on Mum. Andrew nodded and smiled. They were fun to play with. 'I'm going to have a baby. That's why I feel sick at the moment,' said Mum.

'Are you going to be ill all the time?'

'No,' answered Mum.

Andrew saw his mum was tired, and realised

that he must help her while Dad and James were out at work and school. He wasn't going to be selfish any more. James opened the kitchen door and called, 'Hello'.

'We're in the sitting room,' said Mum.

Andrew rushed up to James. 'We've got to be nice to Mum. She's having a baby.'

James sat down and opened the biscuit tin. He took out a biscuit and chewed it.

'Are you pleased?' asked Mum.

James looked at Andrew. 'Could the baby be like him?' he asked.

'Yes,' replied Mum.

'Oh,' said James slowly, then he laughed. 'I'll get used to it! May I play with your train set, Andrew?'

'No!' snapped Andrew. He was only going to be kind to his mum. Then he remembered Jesus was kind to *everybody*.

'OK,' he sighed.

'Great,' said James, running up the stairs.

It was hard being good. Andrew knew he would need a lot of help from God.

Splash

Andrew's mum was going to have a baby soon. She had to rest in the afternoons now because she was tired. She and Andrew used to go out visiting friends. Andrew was fed up. Lots of Andrew's friends and their mums asked him around to play. He would say to his mum, 'Are you coming too?'

'No, darling.'

'I want to stay with you.' Andrew was worried something might happen to his mum while he was out.

One afternoon David came round with Brenda, his mum.

'Can Andrew come swimming with me?' asked David. Andrew smiled and ran to find his swimming trunks and a towel. Then he remembered about his mum.

'Are you going to come?' he asked her.

Mum laughed, 'If I jump into the swimming pool there won't be any room for you.'

Andrew put down his swimming things.

'Oh, please come,' said Brenda.

'What about Mum? I can't leave her,' said Andrew.

'Yes, you can,' smiled Mum.

'No!' replied Andrew firmly.

'I know,' said Brenda to Andrew's mum. 'Let's go to the small pool which belongs to that nice hotel. You can sit by the side with your feet up.'

'Great,' said Mum.

David jumped into the shallow end of the pool. Andrew watched him playing.

'Come on, it's lovely,' shouted David.

Andrew wasn't sure.

'Let me help you,' said David, holding out his hand. Andrew stepped into the water. Brrrr, it was a bit cold. David and Andrew watched Brenda swim up to the deep end.

'I can do that,' said David, flapping his arms and legs about in the water. Andrew loved the way the water splashed everywhere.

'I can do that too,' he said. Soon both boys were soaking wet.

'Be careful!' called Mum from the side. 'You're getting *me* all wet.' Andrew and David giggled.

'Give me a piggy back?' shouted David to his

mum.

'Yes,' answered Brenda, swimming back to the shallow end. Andrew looked sadly up at his mum sitting underneath a large sun umbrella.

'It's no use looking at me, Andrew. I can't give you a piggy back!'

'I'll give you both a ride,' smiled Brenda.

David and Andrew jumped onto Brenda's back and they glided through the water laughing and splashing up and down the pool.

'That's enough, I'm tired,' gasped Brenda. The two boys got off her back and played jumping into the water at the shallow end. This was easy, thought Andrew. He'd been frightened to begin with. Now he wasn't, he could go anywhere he liked.

Andrew waded across to the end of the shallow pool and stood on the little wall which divided the shallow and deep ends. He jumped off the wall, the water went over his head and he began to sink. Andrew opened his mouth to scream but it filled with water, there was water in his ears and up his nose, he couldn't breathe. He flapped his arms but he was still sinking. All of a sudden an arm went round him and pulled him into the fresh air and sunlight. He clutched it very tightly. Brenda carried him to the side of the pool where Mum wrapped him in a towel. He hadn't been under the water for long but to him it seemed ages.

'Why didn't *you* get me out?' Andrew asked

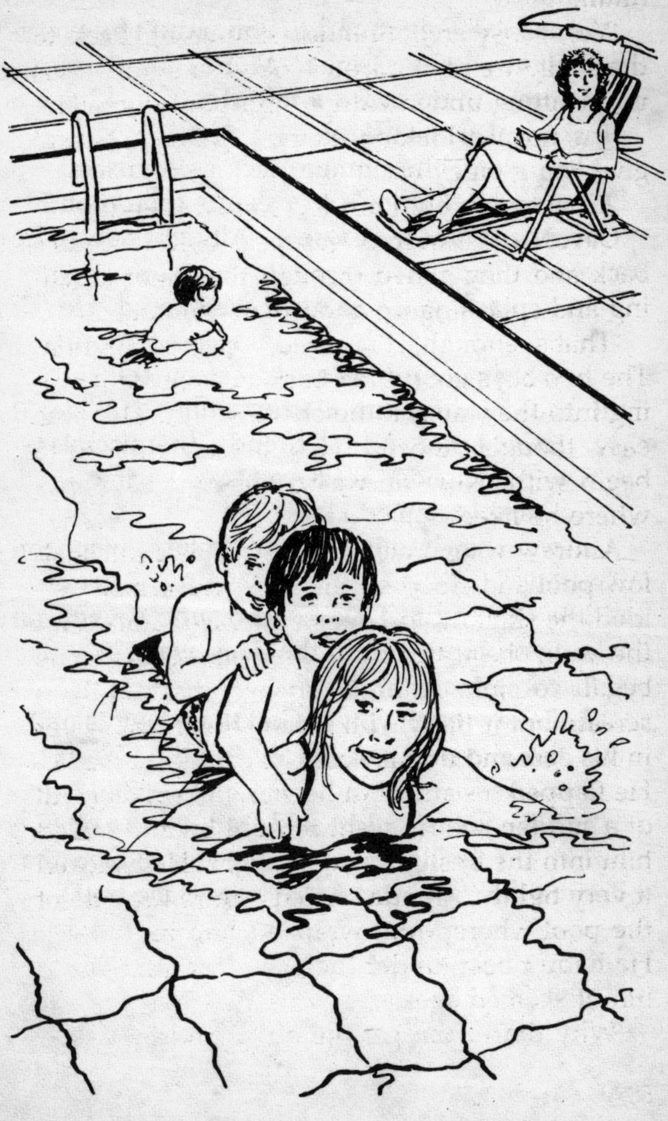

his mum.

'Brenda was right next to you. I can't be everywhere, you know,' sighed Mum.

Andrew thought for a minute. 'Can I have a drink please?' he asked.

Slurp went the orange juice as it rushed up David's and Andrew's straws into their mouths.

Brenda smiled at Andrew. 'All right now?' she asked.

'Yes, thank you,' Andrew whispered. He felt silly.

At bedtime Andrew's dad sat on the side of the bed, reading him a story from the Bible. It was about Jesus and his friends, the disciples.

'I've got friends,' said Andrew.

'So have I,' smiled Dad.

'I went swimming with David,' went on Andrew.

'I know,' replied Dad. 'And who saved you when you jumped into the deep water?'

'David's mum.'

'Let's say thank you to God that David's mum was there to pull you out.'

'No,' said Andrew.

'I think you should,' said Dad.

'No, I'm going to say thank you to God that Brenda *my friend* was there to pull me out!'

The baby

Andrew's mum lay resting upstairs on the bed. Dad put the kettle on, and made Mum a cup of tea. Andrew ran upstairs to see her.

'The baby is going to come today,' she said.

'I'll hold your hand,' said Andrew.

Dad walked in with the tea. 'I think you should go next door to see Sarah and Rachel. James has gone to see his friend Stuart.'

'I want to be here when the baby comes,' said Andrew.

A car stopped outside, and Joan the midwife got out. She was going to look after Andrew's mum when she had the baby. Andrew's mum and dad had decided that the baby was going to be born at home.

'Hello, Andrew,' smiled Joan.

Andrew felt shy. He looked at his feet and didn't answer.

'Woof, woof.'

'Who's that?' said Andrew, running to the window. It was Amber and Hollie, the two golden retriever dogs from next door. Margaret, Rachel and Sarah's mum, was holding their leads.

'Andrew, come with us for a walk,' called Rachel, who was nine. Andrew turned to his mum. 'Will you be all right?' he asked.

'I think so,' Mum replied. 'Dad will look after me.' Andrew ran downstairs and put on his wellies.

It was fun running up the hill with Sarah and her younger sister Rachel.

'Wait for me,' panted Margaret. Amber and Hollie were pulling hard on their leads.

'This is my favourite walk,' smiled Sarah.

'I like the conker trees,' said Rachel.

'The horse chestnut trees you mean,' said Sarah.

'Same thing,' said Rachel.

'I've found one,' laughed Andrew, picking up a conker.

'Ugh, it's from last year. It will be all wormy,' replied Rachel.

Amber and Hollie caught up with Andrew, and licked his wellies. Margaret let the dogs off their leads at the top of the hill. Hollie chased Amber for the stick Amber was holding in her mouth. Margaret, Andrew, Sarah and Rachel, sat down on the grass and watched them for a while.

'There's our house,' said Margaret, looking down the hill. 'Next to yours, Andrew.'

'I wonder how Mum is?' sighed Andrew.

Margaret looked at his sad face. 'Will you help me make a jelly when we get home, Andrew?'

'Yes, please!' shouted Andrew, as he jumped up and tried to pull the stick away from Amber.

When they got back, Rachel and Sarah took Andrew into the bathroom to wash his hands.

'If you're going to make a jelly, your hands have got to be clean,' said Rachel.

In the kitchen Margaret was trying to decide which flavour of jelly to have. Sarah, Rachel and Andrew walked in, and picked up the different packets of jelly.

'I like strawberry,' said Sarah.

'We always have strawberry,' grumbled Rachel.

'What about raspberry?' said Andrew.

'Right, we'll have one raspberry jelly, and one gooseberry jelly,' said Margaret.

Andrew sat on a high stool in Margaret's kitchen, carefully pulling apart the cubes of jelly and placing them in a glass jug. He liked it in Margaret's house. He thought about his mum and dad next door with Joan, the midwife. Amber whimpered for a jelly cube.

'Can I give Amber a bit?' asked Andrew.

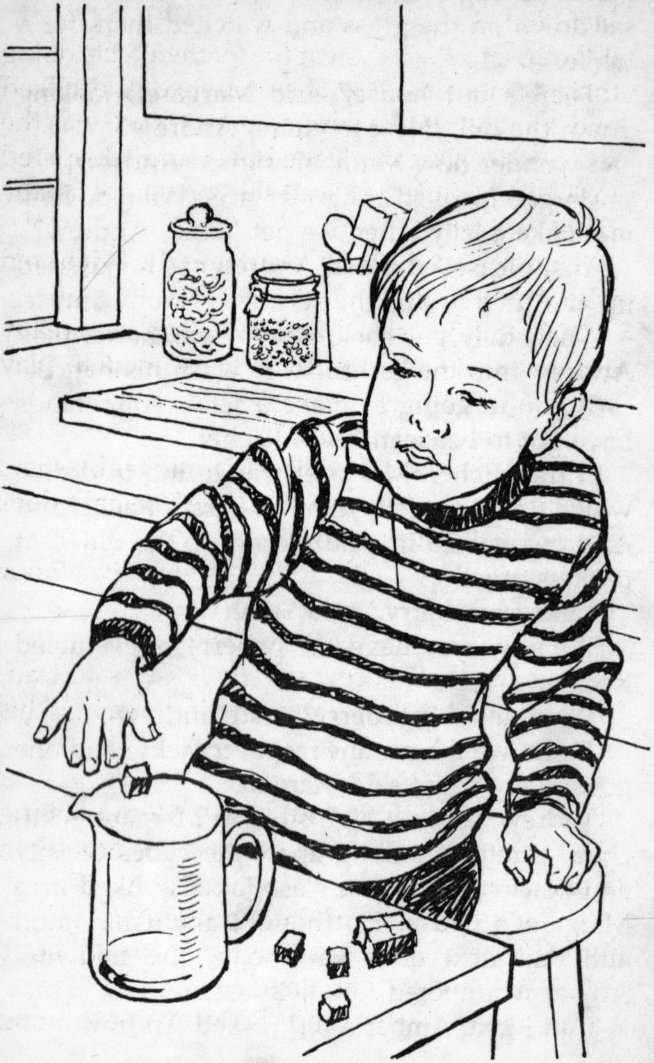

'No, I'll give her a biscuit,' answered Margaret.

Sarah and Rachel sat at the kitchen table doing their school projects. They laughed and talked and sometimes they argued over whose was the red pencil. Margaret leaned over and whispered to Andrew, 'Just you wait till you've got a baby sister or brother.'

'Umm,' said Andrew, staring at the bright red jelly cubes.

'It'll be fun,' said Margaret. 'You've already got an older foster brother. He's good to play with, isn't he?'

'I suppose so,' said Andrew.

He thought of all his friends' younger brothers and sisters. They weren't too bad. The back door opened, and there stood Dad.

'Come and see Alexander Robert King, your new baby brother,' smiled Dad.

'Can we see him?' asked Rachel.

'Yes, just let Andrew see him first,' said Dad, picking Andrew up, and putting him on his shoulders.

'He looks just like you,' said Mum, kissing Andrew. Andrew looked down at his brother in wonder.

'Is he ours, to keep?' he whispered.

'Yes, darling,' smiled Mum.

James said, 'He's so tiny.'

Margaret, Rachel and Sarah crept in and

thought the baby was smashing. Andrew turned to Margaret and said, 'Can I still have my tea at your house?'

That night Andrew lay in his bed listening to the baby crying in the room below. When the baby is older we can play together at the bottom of the garden, he thought. I'll teach him to climb the tree. He was pleased he had a brother.

'Thank you, God,' he said.